Sheina
From Shame to Grace

Margo Holmes

Sheina: From Shame to Grace
Copyright © 2020 by Margo Holmes

ISBN: 978-1-949297-41-6
LCCN: 2020917272

All rights reserved. No part of this publication may be reproduced, stored in a retrieval system, or transmitted in any form or by any means—electronic, mechanical, photocopy, recording, or any other —except for brief quotations in printed or online reviews, without permission in writing from the publisher or author.

This is a fictional story based on the scriptures found in John 4:4-42.

To contact the author Margo Holmes, visit her website: *www.margoholmes.com*, or send an email to: *Godsgreatlove4you@gmail.com*

You may purchase copies of this book from the author or the publisher. Retailers and wholesalers should contact our distributors. Refer to our website for distribution information, as well as an online catalog of all books published by Deeper Revelation Books and its three sub-divisions, including Pure Heart Publications.

Published by the fiction division of Deeper Revelation Books
PURE HEART PUBLICATIONS
Stories that change lives

P.O. Box 4260, Cleveland, TN 37320
Phone: 423-478-2843
Email: *info@deeperrevelationbooks.org*
Website: *www.deeperrevelationbooks.org*

Deeper Revelation Books, and its divisions, assists Christian writers in publishing and distributing their works. Our authors are the ultimate decision-makers in the process. Final responsibility for the creative design, content, permissions, editorial accuracy, stories and doctrinal views, either expressed or implied, belongs to the author. What you hold in your hand is an expression of this author's passion to publish the truth to this generation with a spirit of excellence.

SHEINA is a fictional story based on the scriptures found in John 4:4-30.

The message contained in this book has been etched upon my heart for many years. I want to thank my amazing editor, Mike Shreve, for all he has done to polish it and present it in a form I can share with others. I dedicate it to my sister, Judy, and to my husband, Bill, who understands my heart and whose love for me is as boundless and unconditional as that of my Savior, Christ Jesus.

Contents

Chapter 1
Sheina
 - *From Shame to Grace* 9

Chapter 2
Hadad
 - *Uncommitted in His Youth* 13

Chapter 3
Ram
 - *Cruel in His Jealousy* 19

Chapter 4
Beor
 - *Hateful in His Hope for an Heir* 25

Chapter 5
Nathan
 - *Corrupt in His Lust for Wealth* 29

Chapter 6
Jarib
- The User 33

Chapter 7
Reuben
- Neither Taker, Nor Giver 37

Chapter 8
The Stranger at the Well 41

Chapter 9
Christ
- The Well Of Salvation 45

Chapter 10
Come See Jesus 49

My Prayer 51

About the Author 53

Sheina

1

Sheina
From Shame to Grace

It was time to go to the well. It was time to draw the water. Reaching for the water pot, Sheina set out for Jacob's well. Walking slowly, almost dragging her feet, her mind went back to her youth, back to the first day her mother sent her out on the same, every-day trip to the well. That day felt so different from today. That day, she was excited to be trusted and eager to escape the continuous clamoring of her many brothers and sisters. Her feet almost flew over the familiar trail, packed hard from recent rains and extremely hot days. Too soon, Sheina realized she was already at the well. Faithful not to dally, as she had earlier been admonished by her mother, she quickly filled the pot.

Having completed her task, Sheina knew she should head back down the path to her family's crude dwelling crowded with frustrated parents, whining children and a crying baby.

Because she was the eldest among her siblings, her mother expected her to supervise the constant fights that sprang up between her younger brothers. She also depended on her to help with the never-ending cooking and the grueling chore of washing the family's clothing. That was during the daylight hours.

At night, when her baby sister would wail, Sheina's exhausted mother would call for her. No matter how tired she was from her own difficult day, she had no choice but to rise from her sleeping mat and make her way to the infant. It was quite a challenge to step quickly and carefully through the crowded space and not wake her father. The poor man worked for a cruel master and was barely able to make it through each day. Gently lifting the tiny bundle, she would do whatever was necessary to soothe the colicky babe until she was once again slumbering peacefully. Sometimes that took hours.

Day or night, her life held no privacy and rarely a moment's rest. When her mother made the surprising announcement that for the first time, she would be the one to go draw water from the well, she didn't hesitate. To her, this new assignment felt like an adventure!

As quickly as she could grab the water pot, she was on her way. The well wasn't far and because it was so early, none of the other villagers had yet arrived on the scene. How sweet the silence felt! Most young girls would have been frightened by the solitude, but it was a delight to her. Deciding she could risk a few more moments to relish her liberty and soak in the pleasant, subtle sounds of nature, she took the water pot and settled herself against the trunk of a nearby oak tree. She was thankful for its wide girth that provided good support and cooling shade. Inhaling the fresh morning air, she couldn't remember ever feeling so relaxed.

2

Hadad
Uncommitted in His Youth

Then suddenly, Sheina heard laughter. It sounded almost magical, as if it had been bottled up and just released for an expectant, waiting audience. Having seen no one, she was perplexed by what she heard. Then, as if loosed from the branches of the tree she leaned against, a young man landed so near to her, he scattered clumps of earth at her feet. Startled, she stood up, instinctively clutching her headscarf close to her face. Normally, she would have been afraid. However, before fear could truly set in, she saw such a happy, carefree fellow before her that she, too, began to laugh, joining in and sharing the glee.

That was the day Sheina lost her heart to Hadad.

She soon learned that Hadad was part of a wealthy family. Because the family had servants to take care of their every need, not much was expected of him. Most days his daring nature sent him roaming the countryside to see what new mischief he could explore. That was the pattern of his life until he discovered Sheina. From that day forward, without fail, early every morning, he could be found at the well, waiting eagerly for her appearance.

This went on for several months during which their very public, yet emotionally-charged meetings were always cut short by Sheina's need to return home quickly. Her mother would not be happy if she was kept waiting for the very essential water. With each parting, Hadad grew increasingly impatient, desiring more time with this lovely girl. Sheina grew equally anxious to be away from her life of drudgery. Their yearnings kept increasing until one day they agreed to approach their families about setting a date for their wedding.

Sheina's family, easily won over by Hadad's charm and impressed with his heritage, consented right away to the young couple's request to marry. Because of Sheina's lower station in life, Hadad's parents took more convincing, but they finally relented, and the marriage took place.

As was the custom, the bride joined the household of her husband. For the first few weeks, Sheina's days were filled with the joy of loving Hadad. But then, restlessness began to grow in Hadad, and he began to spend more and more time away from their home. Instead of focusing on her, he began hanging out with his always-rollicking, roguish friends.

As the months wore on and the situation worsened, Sheina's disappointment and loneliness became so acute that she even considered pleading with her family to let her return to their home. Her life may have been miserable there, but at least she was acknowledged and even valued for the help she provided. Not a single person in Hadad's family ever included her in so much as a casual conversation. The servants had evidently been warned to keep their distance as well.

From the beginning, Hadad was seldom around during the day. Then he started staying away in the evenings. He never even sent word where he was or what he was doing. She felt completely abandoned. Sadly, she learned where he was spending some of those evenings. It was with other women, women who were well known for being loose with their morals. She was shocked! How foolish and naïve she had been to rashly marry someone who would completely disregard the commandment of the Lord not to commit adultery. She realized now, too late, that she should have prayed. She should have sought the Lord, asking Him if Hadad was the mate He had chosen for her.

One afternoon, to help take her mind off the situation, Sheina decided to see if the fruit she loved the most, the Jaffa orange, was ripe enough for picking. Taking up the round, sturdy basket she had recently woven, she headed for the grove. It was there, as she was picking the fruit, Ram, one of Hadad's more settled friends showed up.

Sheina was completely unaware that Ram had been watching her for weeks, waiting for an opportunity to seek her out. For some time, he had been secretly harboring the thought that he could possess this stunning, though neglected young woman for himself.

Cautiously making a show of deep respect, Ram approached Sheina. He began speaking of her beauty and of his admiration for her faithfulness to Hadad, in spite of Hadad's reckless, self-absorbed behavior. Suddenly, something gave way inside Sheina. Her heart that was broken poured forth its sorrow. As the tears streamed down her face, Ram tenderly wrapped her in his arms. He declared a love that would be true, a love that would be constant, a love that would be a "day-in and day-out," all-the-time kind of love.

As he had hoped, Sheina yielded to his proclamations of the kind of love that she had imagined and still desperately longed for. She became convinced that kind of love could still become a reality. She needed only to accept what Ram was offering.

Unfortunately, Sheina, though hesitant, repeated what was certainly another emotional, hasty, and unwise decision. Together, she and Ram went to find Hadad and reason with him to release Sheina from their marriage.

When they finally located and approached her wayward husband, he seemed irritated by the interruption which caused the conversation to go much easier than either Sheina or Ram anticipated. Strangely, Hadad did not exhibit a bit of anger or resentment toward either one of them. Instead, he seemed relieved, dismissing his wife and his friend with the same nonchalant attitude that overshadowed his usual approach to life.

3

Ram
Cruel in His Jealousy

And so, Sheina became the wife of Ram. Sheina liked being a wife. She enjoyed the security and the sameness of each day as she went about her duties. Wanting with all her heart to please Ram, she worked hard at being an excellent companion. Therefore, Sheina was taken by surprise when Ram began complaining. It was first about little things, like a few weeds in the garden or a meal that didn't turn out well. Then his discontent was triggered by so many things, and Sheina didn't know what to think. It was especially hurtful when Ram complained about her appearance. Ram had always talked of her great beauty. But then, Ram began to rage about her changing body, insisting that the baby probably belonged to Hadad.

Sheina, bewildered by her husband's change of heart and new volatile personality, tried her best to calm and reassure him. But when she did, Ram grew violent. He beat Sheina, and he beat her badly. Sheina did not go out for many days, waiting for the injuries to heal. Finally, she had no choice.

A trip had to be made to the market. Self-conscious, she attempted to cover the bruises that still remained, but she could not conceal them all.

As Sheina made her usual purchase at the first booth that was crammed with bins brimming with grains of every sort, the vendor began to make conversation with her. That was out of the ordinary. He was normally curt with buyers, wanting to free himself up to be available for the next customer who might approach, so that he could make more sales.

At first, Sheina was embarrassed by his attention and wanted to walk away, politely yet swiftly. However, something, perhaps her troubled and confused state of mind, compelled her to linger. It helped, too, that the market was crowded, and conversations were buzzing loudly all around her, causing her to feel less conspicuous.

Before she could discreetly avoid the conversation, the vendor began questioning Sheina about her bruises. His sympathetic attitude was irresistible. With his soft voice, he created a sense of calm around her shattered emotions.

Pouring out her heart, Sheina shared with Beor, the vendor, her fear that the child she was carrying had been conceived when she was still married to Hadad.

Sheina confessed how frightened she was that the child might resemble Hadad and not her husband, Ram, and that Ram's fury, already blazing toward her, would be released upon the child. Sheina continued to relate to Beor that she couldn't return to her parents' home. There was no room, and her parents were barely able to provide for the children still under their care.

Beor, attracted to Sheina's beauty and submissive nature, pondered his own situation. He had been praying for a wife. His greatest desire was to have a home full of children, especially a son who would carry on the family name and business. *Perhaps*, he thought, *Sheina could be the answer to my prayers*.

While explaining that he had no wife or children, Beor said it wouldn't matter to him if the child was conceived by Hadad or by Ram. He would not only accept the child into his home, he would accept the child as his rightful heir. He quickly suggested that Sheina leave Ram and become his wife.

Flabbergasted, but feeling desperate, she complied with Beor's plan to offer a "business" transaction to Ram. Displaying amazing courage and confidence, Beor immediately set out to find Ram. Sheina, though awkward with her pregnancy, hid herself as best she could in the back of the grain stall and waited with mounting fear.

Sheina fully expected Ram to storm into the marketplace and force her to come home. However, to her enormous surprise and great relief, Beor returned within the hour with news that Ram no longer wanted his wife or the baby. Instead, he was anxious to line his pockets and readily agreed to the transaction.

Sheina

4

Beor
Hateful in His Hope for an Heir

She now belonged to Beor! She wanted to belong. She didn't mind being considered a "possession." She didn't mind being purchased. She was grateful for a place to birth and safely raise her child. But when the child came, everything changed. Beor was not pleased with little Phoebe. His great hope had been set on a son.

Beor was not physically cruel to Sheina or Phoebe, he simply ignored them. Except for the times when he approached Sheina concerning his desire for a son, Beor seldom acknowledged either of them as part of his life.

As months turned into years, there was no heir, and because there was also no love, one day, Beor brought home another woman. Once again, Sheina had married without seeking the counsel of the Lord. As a result, here she was, married to a man who from the beginning had his own personal agenda. There was no concern or regard for her well-being. What kind of marriage was that? Surely, it was not what the Lord would have chosen for her.

Sheina was not able to adjust. Anguish consumed her. Rarely did she eat and seldom did she rise from her bed. Then, one day, sweet Phoebe, desperate to see her mother recover her will to live, brought her favorite uncle to see Sheina.

Nathan knelt beside the bed, covering her hands with his own. He began relating the dilemma he was facing. He needed someone to care for his aging parents.

Nathan assured Sheina that he would not expect her to love him. His sincere desire was for them to help each other. She would have a place where she could live and not have to see that "other woman" every day, especially since she was pregnant with Beor's child. Also, Nathan would know his parents would be well cared for.

At first, Sheina did not respond. Then, she heard the sobs of deep anguish escape from Phoebe's chest. Watching her mother's life being overtaken by severe depression had taken a toll on Phoebe. It had stolen her joy, her hope, even her freedom. She was afraid to leave her mother alone. As long as her mother was trapped in her sorrow, so was Phoebe.

Finally, Phoebe's sobs broke through to Sheina. She sat up and began to speak. Sheina declared to Nathan that she would go to his house and care for his parents. While doing so, she would finish raising her precious daughter.

Sheina

5

Nathan
Corrupt in His Lust for Wealth

And so, Sheina became the wife of Nathan. It was her fourth marriage. She felt guilty. She knew the commandments, for the Samaritans were part Jewish. "You shall not commit adultery"—how that mandate from God rang in her heart and mind constantly. But she felt trapped in a vicious cycle and could not see any way of escape, so she just pushed those haunting words out. God could never love her anyway (or so she convinced herself).

Sheina resigned herself over to her lot in life, but she decided she would still try to do her best within the confines of her circumstances. In a short period of time, she became an expert at caring for Nathan's parents, whom she genuinely came to love. Thankfully, they loved her back.

Nathan seemed grateful. He treated Sheina well and even lavished gifts on her and Phoebe.

For a while, life was good, very good, until that fatal day. She never saw it coming. She had no idea that Nathan's character or actions were anything less than admirable. He certainly would never be guilty of corruption or dishonest business practices.

It started out as an ordinary day. The weather was perfect; it was crisp but sunny. Sheina and Phoebe decided to take a stroll in the family's vineyard. When they returned, Nathan was gone. Not only gone but gone forever. The authorities, at the request of a disgruntled associate, had unexpectedly come to question Nathan concerning several suspicious transactions. Nathan, normally levelheaded and in complete control, became so agitated and overwrought, he suffered a massive heart attack and died instantly.

Nathan's older brother, Jarib, was already on the scene. After curtly describing the events to Sheina, he began issuing orders to the household. He informed them that he was willing to take on the responsibility of his brother's property and family, which, of course, included Sheina.

Sheina's heart sank. Sheina knew enough about her husband's brother to expect the worst. He was an overbearing, selfish and secretive tyrant. She had witnessed more than once how he treated his family and his servants, lashing out at them for the least infraction. It seemed to Sheina that Jarib possessed no compassion, indeed, no feelings or conscience whatsoever.

All Sheina could think, all she could feel, all she could say to Phoebe was, *"Whatever will we do? Oh, Phoebe, I am so sorry. I don't know a way out!"* And so, Sheina became the wife of Jarib.

6

Jarib
The User

Fortunately, soon after Sheina became the wife of Jarib (her fifth husband), Phoebe, still young but remarkably mature, met Caleb. Caleb was kind and steady. Although he came from a poor family, Caleb was unusually gifted as a carpenter, making him a good provider. Best of all, Caleb loved sweet Phoebe with all of his heart. That fall, Phoebe became Caleb's bride.

Sheina was still the wife of Jarib. She had been the wife of Hadad, uncommitted in his youth. She had been the wife of Ram, cruel in his jealousy. She had been the wife of Beor, hateful in his hope for an heir. She had been the wife of Nathan, corrupt in his lust for wealth.

Sheina found it difficult to believe at that juncture in her life, she had been married to five husbands. She could not help but think how things might have been different if she had depended more on the Lord and not on those undependable, unpredictable men. If only she had turned her heart and mind fully toward her Creator and sought His comfort and His guidance!

Sheina knew being married to Jarib would not be good, but nothing had prepared her for the depths of the brutal treatment to which she was subjected at his hands. She was damaged daily. The severity of the hurt depended on his mood. If he felt sadistic, he would invite his friends over to treat Sheina with indignities she had never known existed. If he was filled with rage, he would constantly whisper threats into her ears, threats she knew he was capable of carrying out.

Nevertheless, what devastated her most of all was that Jarib would not allow her to see Phoebe. She had heard that Phoebe was soon to birth a child. Oh, how Sheina wanted to be with her daughter, wanted to be a part of her life, wanted to be a grandmother! But she knew as long as she was with Jarib, it would never happen. Things would never change.

Sheina was tired. She was weary of being used. Jarib used her for anything and everything. He used her in ways mundane and imaginable, and he used her in ways savage and unimaginable. Jarib used Sheina until she felt she couldn't be used anymore. One day, Sheina just left. She left the house, walked to town and didn't go back.

Reuben
Neither Taker, Nor Giver

Because Sheina had not made a conscious decision to leave Jarib, she arrived in town with only a few personal items stuffed into a sack.

Exhausted from the mental anguish as well as the long walk, she collapsed against a stone wall. Leaning back, she closed her eyes and simply rested.

While doing so, it occurred to her that she had no plan. She had no idea where she could live or how she would eat. Almost paralyzed with hopelessness, she remained slumped against the wall.

About an hour had passed when she felt someone nudge her foot. Looking up, she saw a man she knew. It was Reuben. Reuben was well known. He lived in almost the very center of town and was often hired by local landowners to work on various projects. More than once he had been hired by Jarib. Therefore, Reuben had been an eyewitness to Sheina's situation. Observing her disheveled appearance and being a man of few words, he didn't hit her with a barrage of questions. All he said was, *"You can stay with me if you like."*

As usual, Sheina saw no other way. She moved in with Reuben. Reuben had been single all his life, never really committing to any person or to any job. He was satisfied with his simple, uncomplicated life. He didn't expect much from himself or anyone else. Reuben asked Sheina to cook the meals. She could do that. He asked Sheina to take the water pot and go to the well. She could do that. So, there she was, with the water pot and on her way, once again, down the path to Jacob's well.

8

The Stranger at the Well

Lifting her head as she rounded the bend, Sheina saw a man sitting by the well. *Should I still draw the water*, she thought. Sheina was so tired, too tired to make another trip, and they needed the water. She decided to go to the other side. Perhaps, if she kept her eyes averted and moved as quietly as she could, she would not call attention to herself.

Then Sheina heard the voice and the request, *"Give me a drink."* She was shocked. The man was obviously a Jew. Why would He even address her? The Jews had nothing to do with the Samaritans.

He then began to tell Sheina that if she would only recognize the gift of God, if she would only recognize who He was, that He could give her living water! Baffled, she observed that the man did not even have a vessel to draw with. So, Sheina questioned Him, saying, *"Sir, the well is deep, how can You provide me with living water?"*

The man answered, *"All who drink of the water from this well will thirst again. But whoever takes a drink of the water that I will give him shall never thirst. Indeed, the water that I give shall become in him a spring of water welling up to everlasting life."*

A spring of water! Everlasting life! That sounded wonderful to Sheina. How very thirsty her soul was! How weary she was of the continuous trips to the well. Enduring the comments of the men, the whispers among the women and even the scattering of the children hurt more than all the years of abuse she had suffered.

Filled with hope and longing, Sheina made her request to the stranger, *"Sir, give me this water, so that I never thirst again and do not have to come here continually to draw water."*

The stranger replied, *"Go, call your husband and come back here."* Of course, technically, she had no husband. Jarib had quickly divorced her, and there was no way that Reuben would even pretend he was such. Filled with shame, Sheina confessed to the stranger that she had no husband.

Then He said, *"You are right. As a matter of fact, you have had five husbands, and the man you live with now is not your husband."* The stranger stated this simply, with no show of emotion, judgment, or condemnation. Still, humiliation flooded her soul.

How did the stranger know? How did He know Sheina was living with Reuben? How did He know she'd had five husbands? Surely, she was talking to a prophet! If so, He could settle something she had been puzzled about for quite some time.

"Sir, our fathers worshipped on this mountain, Mount Gerizim; yet you say Jerusalem is where men ought to worship."

Finally, her confusion was confessed . . . to a Jew who had been treating her with genuine kindness, all the while knowing everything about her. Would He even continue talking with her?

The stranger spoke again, *"Woman, believe me, a time is coming when you will worship the Father, not just on a mountain or in Jerusalem. You Samaritans do not know what you are worshipping. Salvation is coming from the Jews. Indeed, it is already here. True worshippers will worship the Father in spirit and in truth. The Father is seeking such a people to be His worshippers. God is a Spirit and those who worship Him must worship Him in spirit and in truth."*

Sheina

9

Christ
The Well Of Salvation

Trying to process the whole encounter and fully understand all the words spoken by the stranger, Sheina continued speaking out loud what was running through her mind. She said, *"I know that the Messiah is coming, and I know that when He comes, He will explain everything to us."*

To this the stranger declared, *"I who speak to you am He."*

As Sheina heard the words coming forth, hope sprang up. Hope that this stranger was who He said He was. Hope that He was the gift of God, that He was the Messiah, the Anointed One! Hope that He was that well of water springing up into eternal life.

Just then, a group of men came on the scene. Sheina could tell the men had come to join the stranger, but not one of them made any comment or said a word to her.

Not knowing what to do, Sheina just stood still waiting. As she did, she heard one of the men address the stranger. He called Him *"Jesus."*

Sheina

10

Come See Jesus!

Now fully convinced the stranger was who He said He was, Sheina forgot all about her water pot that was propped against the wall of the well. She began to run, as swiftly as she had run as a child, back to town to tell all the people: *"Come see a man who told me everything that I ever did! Can this be the Christ? Come! Come quickly to see! They call him Jesus. He's at the well. Come now!"*

The people, so stunned at the transformation in Sheina's countenance, couldn't help but pay attention. The people who rarely heard her speak above a whisper, with her head always bowed in shame, saw a face lifted up and shining with joy.

And the voice they heard was filled with boldness! What they saw and heard now was a woman unabashedly determined to share with the entire town this new discovery, this proof, this good news they had been waiting for. The people of the town were so persuaded by the testimony of Sheina that they began running, following her down the familiar, well-traveled path to the well. They wanted to see if the stranger she spoke about really was Christ, if He was their long-awaited Messiah.

Even Reuben, the man Sheina had been living with, set out with the others. Even Reuben, who seemed to simply drift through life, never questioning, never searching, or yearning for more, set out running to the well.

Even he wanted to see if this stranger who had caused such a change in Sheina was the Christ he had heard about. Even he wanted to drink more than the water Sheina could bring back from Jacob's well. Even Reuben wanted to drink from the wells of salvation. And so it is for all who have ever read His words and heard His voice—throughout the world and in every generation. He is still saying, *"Come to Me and drink!"*

"For God sent not his Son into the world to condemn the world; but that the world through him might be saved."
(John 3:17, KJV)

My Prayer

My prayer is that through this story you have begun to develop a heart that will not be quick to judge or to condemn, but you will have a heart filled with compassion that is eager to love and ready to save. The life of "the woman at the well" may not have been exactly as portrayed in this small book, but then again, maybe it was very similar. My main purpose has been to offer a different narrative of her story. Maybe, just maybe, she should not be labeled as an immoral woman. Maybe, just maybe, she was a hurting, used, abused, battered, disappointed, grief-stricken, and humiliated person that desperately needed the love of Jesus. Think about it!

–author, Margo Holmes

About the Author...

Margo Holmes resides in Lake Placid, Florida with her husband, Bill. She is the author of the wonderful children's series titled *God's Great Love*. Margo's joy-filled spirit overflows in doing the work of God, spending time with her family (especially her fifteen grandchildren and one great-granddaughter), and playing the game of tennis.
www.margoholmes.com

About the Illustrator...

Monica Turner is a central Florida native. She and her family reside in Sebring, Florida on a small ranch. Homeschooling her four children and painting commissioned art for clients, from Canada to Australia, keeps Monica busy. Two of the colorful murals in the town of Lake Placid are her beautiful creations. Most of her work is of Florida's rich wildlife, farm life, cowboy culture, and animal portraiture. Her favorite scripture passage is Psalm 91. For custom art you may contact Monica at *gowild@MonicaTurnerArt.com*

Additional Resources

Margo Holmes has also authored a nine-book children's series titled **GOD'S GREAT LOVE**. The first book introduces children to God's love and the gift of salvation. The other books cover important subjects that help lay a strong faith-foundation in the life of any child.

1. God's Great Love
2. Why Be Baptized?
3. Understanding Communion
4. Teach Us to Pray
5. Follow Me
6. Fruit of the Spirit
7. He Is Risen
8. Acts of God and of the Apostles
9. Jesus Is Coming Again!

Margo's oldest granddaughter, Lauren, reading to her youngest granddaughter, Bristol

At the end of each book, there is a special prayer, as well as review questions. These books make excellent gifts for any child. They are ideal for reaching out to children who may never be introduced to the basics of the Gospel otherwise. They are equally valuable as a teaching resource in a classroom or study group.

To learn more about the series, view Margo's television interviews posted on *www.deeperrevelationbooks.org*. You may place an order on her website: *www.margoholmes.com*.